ordinary
terrible
things

Divorce Is the Worst

Death Is Stupid

TELL ME ABOUT SEX, GRANDMA
Written and Illustrated by Anastasia Higginbotham
FP
FEMINIST PRESS
AT THE CITY UNIVERSITY OF NEW YORK
NEW YORK CITY

Published in 2017 by the Feminist Press
at the City University of New York
The Graduate Center
365 Fifth Avenue, Suite 5406
New York, NY 10016

feministpress.org

First printing April 2017

Illustration and design by Anastasia Higginbotham
Photography by Alexa Hoyer
Production by Drew Stevens and Suki Boynton

Special thanks to Sabatino Luongo Higginbotham for painting rainbows, cutting oranges, and inspiring this sparkling child.

Library of Congress Cataloging-in-Publication Data is available for this title.
ISBN 978-1-55861-419-2

Manufactured by Thomson-Shore, Dexter, MI (USA); RMA13HS598, October, 2016

for gono

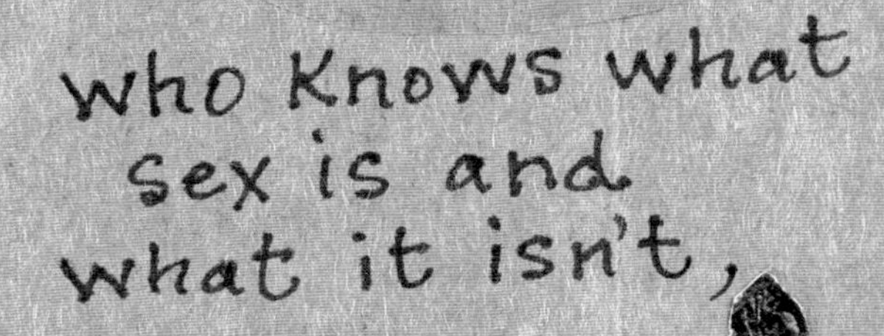

who knows what
sex is and
what it isn't,

and

for Susan and Sharon,
who are healers.

SEX

SEX
Sex is everywhere.
Certified

It is also hidden.

Knowing where to look...

when
you want
to find
answers ...

...is key.

Tell me about sex, Grandma.

Maria Hilf,
Auxilium, B. V. Mariae.

Curiosity about sex
is your birthright.

click!

It's in your nature
to want to know...

Well,
whattaya
wanna
know?

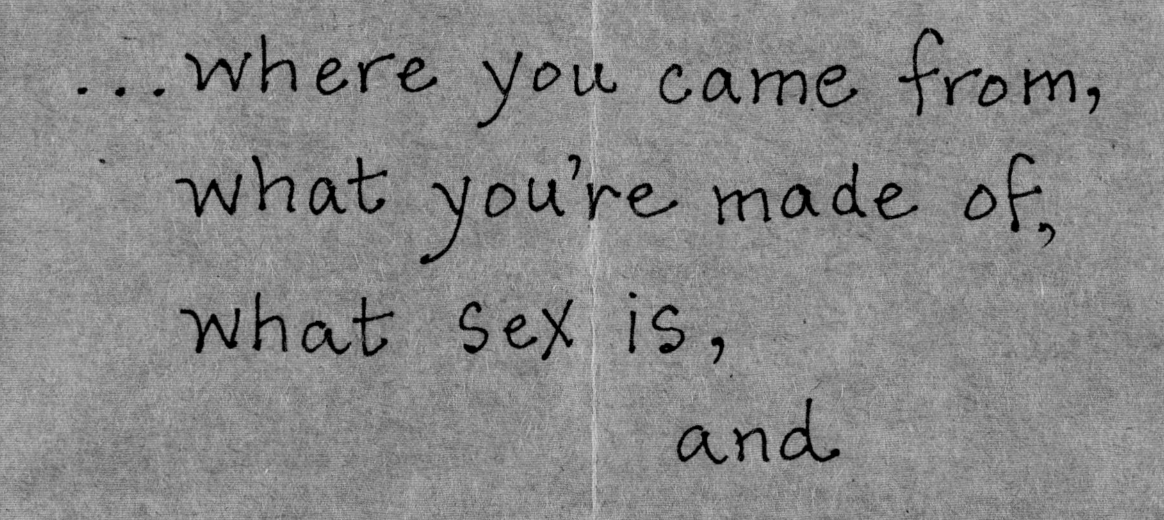
...where you came from,
what you're made of,
what sex is,
and

... what it isn't.

What's so bad about it?

Who says sex is bad?

I'm not supposed to see it, know it, or do it — like a swear or a secret. So it must be bad.

Sex is already part of you.
You were born with it.

It's a grown-up thing.

So's coffee. Nobody cares if I see coffee.

Sex is private.

Just tell me!
Actually, wait. Let me get ready.

– hmmm...
Okay.
I'm ready.
Tell me.

It's a thing with bodies.
Moving so it feels good.
By yourself or
with someone.

How do I know how to move?

The feelings tell you.

Where will I feel them?

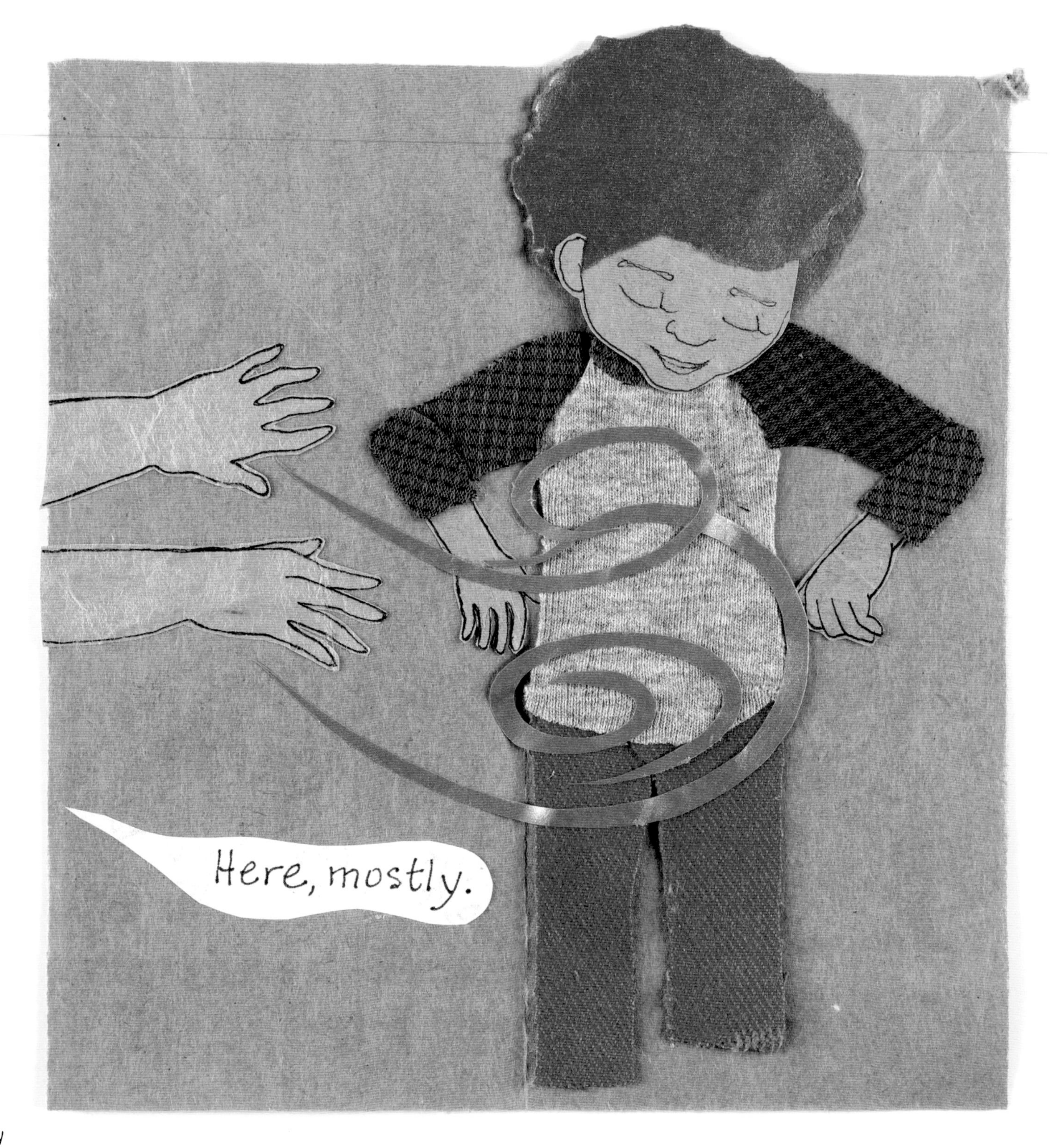
Here, mostly.

The feelings are your sexuality.

Does sex always make a baby?

No, thank goodness.

Why "thank goodness"?

Oh, did I say that out loud?

I'm hungry.
Okay. Let's eat.

The feelings change as
you grow up.
They grow up
with you.

Sex is an energy, an action,
a conversation,
a revelation.*

* sudden burst of understanding or discovery.

Learning about sex is
learning about yourself.

I have a sex thing I do in private— moving so it feels good.
Is that okay?
Yes. It is okay, and best to do only in private.

Your sexuality is
something you discover
as you go along —

how you feel,
what you like,

Sahadi
and who you like.

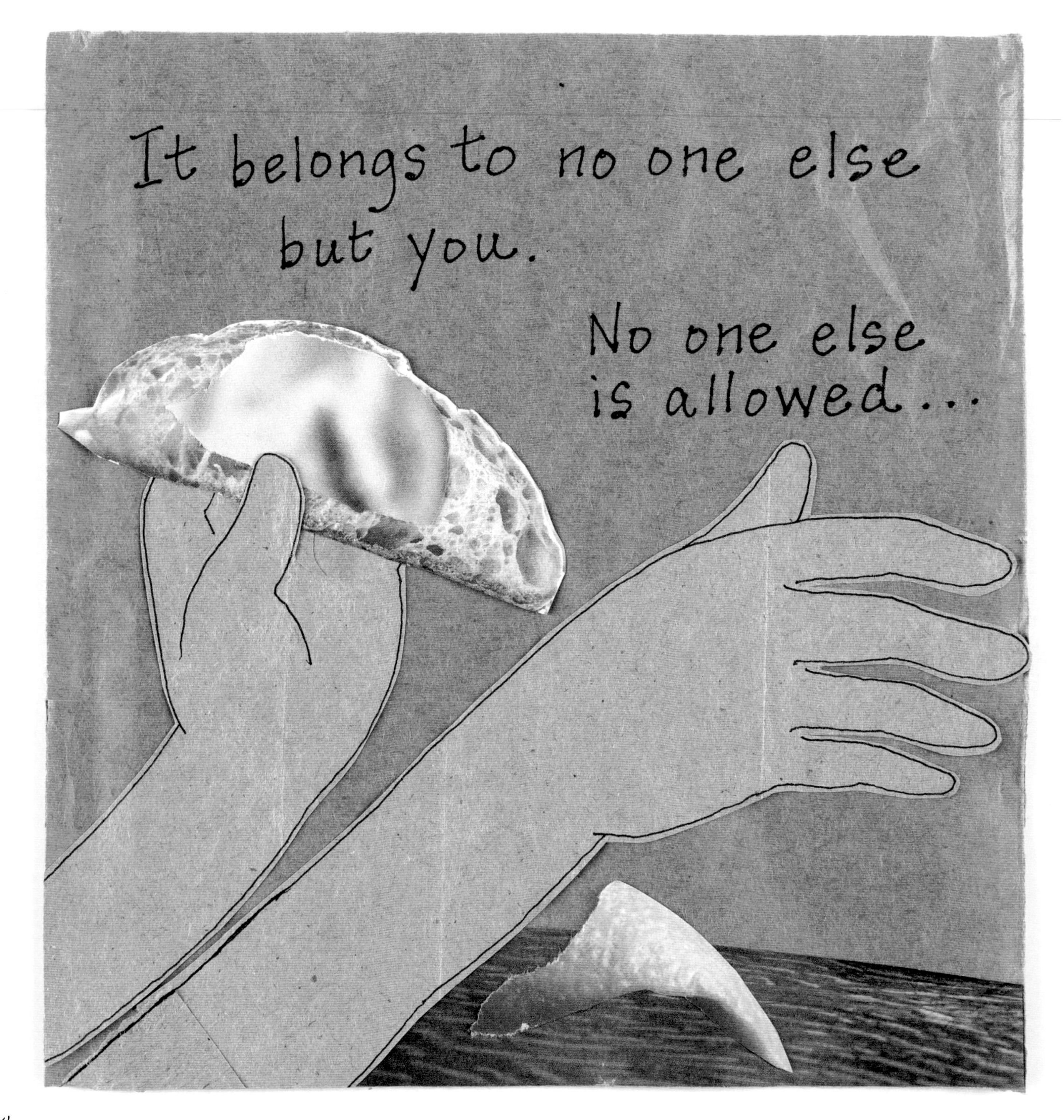
It belongs to no one else but you.
No one else is allowed...

to boss you
into sex, or

take it from you
without your permission.

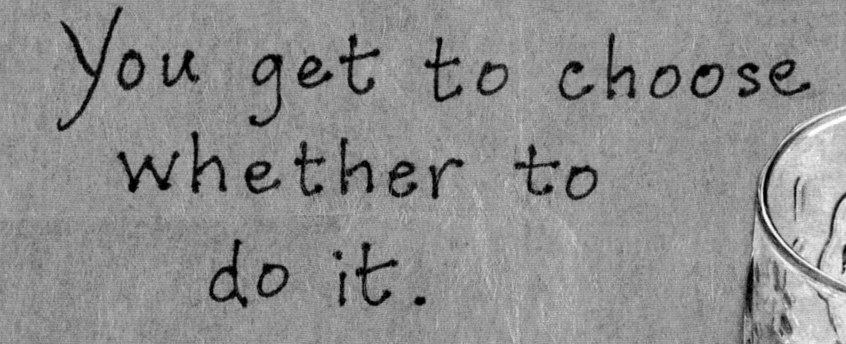

You get to choose
whether to
do it.

More?

Same goes for everyone.
You choose
for you.

They choose
for them.

No, thanks.

But why don't adults want kids to know about sex?
Our job is to protect you.
From sex?
From growing up too fast.

And from people who don't follow the rules.

It is never okay
for an adult to choose
to have sex with a child
— even if they
love and take care
of you.

What rules?

No sex with anyone unless they say they want to, and no sex, ever, with kids.
It's harmful. It's against the law. And anyone who tells you different is lying.

Once those rules are respected, a person's sexuality is no one else's business.

Your sexuality
is yours alone.

Yours to discover.
Yours to treasure.

You want me to give you a push?
Yes.
High?
Yes.
Got your shoes on?
Yes.
Cool. Let's go.
Yours to share if you choose.

Grandma, what did you want to be when you were little?
Big!

Why?
What do you want?

I want to save the oceans!! I want light-up pants! I want a dolphin who only I understand what she is saying!
Wow!

May your choices about sex always be yours to make...

What does your dolphin say to you?

She says, "Thank you for my ocean."

...whether or not you ever decide to do it.

The end.

Wanna guess the most important part of sex?
The choosing part.

Read this next part out loud:

I am the one-and-only, top-boss, in-charge decider about sex in my life for my whole life. Everyone else is the boss of themself too.

When there's a choice to make
– any choice at all –
it helps to know what you
want.
Do you get a feeling of
yes NO
LOOK
here →
stop
go
SLOW ZONE
about any of these images? →

You are already making choices all the time about what you like and...
...what you want. You know a lot.

When your voice can't find the words, pay attention to your body.

tight fist + stomach twist =

No WAY I'm getting on that thing.

Read your own and other people's body language.

Animals' too!

Being still + Breathing easy =

I'm content to just be here right now.

Go to bed.
But...?!
It's bedtime.
Line up!
But...?!
Recess is over.
Try one bite.
But...?!
Do it.
It's always good to know what you want
What about when there is no choice?
even when you may not get it.

Sex is POWERFUL. So are you.

Be aware: There is an abyss* of images out there that can distort and even ruin your experience of learning about sex.

*bottomless pit

Those aren't the answers you're looking for. Move along.

Choose a grown-up who will help you answer your questions safely.

In the meantime and for all time...

Be safe.
Be you.
Be loved.

Anastasia Higginbotham's books about ordinary, terrible things tell stories of children who navigate trouble with their senses sharp and souls intact.

Help may come from family, counselors, teachers, and dreams — but it's the children who find their own way through.

Anastasia has been making books by hand her whole life as a way to cope with change and grow.

You CAN TOO!

ordinary
terrible
things

ord
terr
t

ordinary
terrible
things